MARY K. WHITTINGTON

The Patchwork Lady

Illustrated by JANE DYER

Harcourt Brace Jovanovich, Publishers

San Diego　　New York　　London

Requests for permission to make copies of any part of the work
should be mailed to: Permissions Department,
Harcourt Brace Jovanovich, Publishers, Orlando, Florida 32887.

Library of Congress Cataloging-in-Publication Data
Whittington, Mary K.
The patchwork lady / by Mary K. Whittington: illustrated
by Jane Dyer. — 1st ed.
p.   cm.
Summary: The Patchwork Lady prepares her colorful patchwork
house for her birthday party.
ISBN 0-15-259580-5
[1. Patchwork — Fiction. 2. Birthdays — Fiction.] I. Dyer, Jane,
ill. II. Title.
PZ7.W6188Pat 1991
[E] — dc20   89-24606

First edition   A B C D E

For my parents,

Bill and Jean Whittington

—M.K.W.

For the *other* Jane

—J.D.

The illustrations in this book were done in Winsor & Newton
watercolors on Waterford 140-lb. hot press paper.
The display and text type were set in Kennerly Old Style
by Thompson Type, San Diego, California.
Color separations were made by Bright Arts, Ltd., Singapore.
Printed and bound by Tien Wah Press, Singapore
Production supervision by Warren Wallerstein and Ginger Boyer
Designed by Camilla Filancia
Edited by Jane Yolen

The Patchwork Lady gets up in the morning.
She puts on a plaid dress, argyle stockings,
and checkered slippers.

She brushes her teeth with striped toothpaste
and braids an embroidered ribbon into her hair.

She goes to the kitchen to make breakfast.
The sun streams in through many-paned windows,
throwing squares of light upon her tablecloth.

She makes toast,
white and brown,
with honey and yellow butter dots.

She drinks cranberry tea from her valentine cup
and reads a letter that has just arrived.

"COMPANY," says the Patchwork Lady.

She opens her closet
and pulls out her feather duster
and her carpet sweeper
from crisscrossed bunches
of brooms and mops.

She cleans her living room:
the spiral green-and-purple rug,
the calico couch, the blue-flowered chair.

In her garden the Patchwork Lady fills a basket
with orange roses, white daisies, and violets.

She returns to her house,
no two windows or doors alike,
rainbow walls of brick and wood and stone.

"IS COMING," says the Patchwork Lady.

Up in the attic she unpacks a box of streamers,
but they are gray with dust
and tatter when she touches them.

Inside another box, mice nest in coils
of shredded paper chains.

What should she do?

Then she remembers.
The trunk beneath the window holds scarves of silk:
lilac, pink, and apricot.
She lifts the lid and takes them out.

End to end she knots them.
They float behind her down the stairs
into the living room.

There she hangs them in festoons
from corner to corner,
from curtain rods to chandelier.

Everything looks beautiful,
but will the company like it?

"FOR," says the Patchwork Lady.

In the kitchen she mixes plum punch
with minty ice cubes
and sets out a bowl of strawberries.
She bakes many chocolate cupcakes.

But when she tries to spread them
with marshmallow icing,
they crumble.

What should she do?

At last she has an idea.
She pours golden honey over the crumbs
and presses them together
into an enormous cake.

She ices it and sticks a candle in the middle.
Everything looks delicious,
but will the company think so, too?

"MY," says the Patchwork Lady.

Now everything is ready.
She goes outside and waits on her porch swing
between her spotted cat and her ring-tailed dog.

She knits an afghan of rippling designs, and worries.
What will she do if her company laughs
at her decorations and refreshments?

People are coming down her walk.
They wear dotted swiss, corduroy, and herringbone.

"How glad we are to see you," they say.
"How have you been?" they ask.

But they stop talking when she leads them into the house.
They take one look, and . . .

"Ah," they say. "What wonderful streamers."
"What a luscious-looking cake."

And they give her a big silver box
tied with a crimson bow.

"BIRTHDAY PARTY!" says the Patchwork Lady.